Zeke Meeks

Zeke Meeks is published by
Picture Window Books
A Capstone Imprint
1710 Roe Crest Drive
North Mankato, MN 56003
www.capstonepub.com

MY WORST
NIGHTMARE:
BUGS!

Library of Congress Cataloging Green, D. L. (Debra L.)
  Zeke Meeks vs. the stinkin' science fair / by D.L. Green; illustrated
by Josh Alves.
    p. cm. — (Zeke Meeks)
  Summary: Third-grader Zeke Meeks needs to win the prize in the
science project contest because the class bully is threatening him,
but so far all his ideas are ending in messy disasters—can his friend
Hector save the day?
  ISBN 978-1-4048-6802-1 (library binding)
  ISBN 978-1-4048-7222-6 (pbk.)
  1. Science fairs—Juvenile fiction. 2. Science projects—Juvenile
fiction. 3. Bullying—Juvenile fiction. 4. Friendship—Juvenile fiction.
5. Schools—Juvenile fiction. [1. Science fairs—Fiction. 2. Science
projects—Fiction. 3. Bullies—Fiction. 4. Friendship—Fiction. 5. Schools—
Fiction. 6. Humorous stories.] I. Alves, Josh, ill. II. Title. III. Title:
Zeke Meeks versus the stinkin' science fair. IV. Title: Zeke Meeks vs.
the stinking science fair.

  PZ7.G81926Zi 2012

  813.6—dc23   2011029902

Vector Art Credits: Shutterstock
Book design by K. Fraser   3 9957 00169 9301

I LOOK SO
PRETTY.

Printed in the United States of America in Stevens Point, Wisconsin.
102011   006404WZS12

VERY CONFUSED
BOY DOG.

HE PLAYS DRESS-UP
WITH MY LITTLE SISTER
WAY TOO OFTEN.

Zeke Meeks
vs THE STINKIN' SCIENCE FAIR

ILLUSTRATED BY
JOSH ALVES

BY
D. L. GREEN

Image that makes me sick.
It gives me the cold sweats.

TABLE OF

Quick at making my life a mess!

BOYS RULE EVERYTHING BUT THE PLAYGROUND

Hawaiian Waggles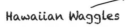

CONTENTS

GIRLS DROOL ALL BUT GRACE – SHE BITES

A WONDERFUL Day,
If You Like
Being Pushed

and
Punished

It was one of the worst days ever in my entire life. It all started during recess on a cold November day in my town of Cheeseham, Massachusetts.

I was on the school playground, playing handball with Hector Cruz. Hector had just moved here. My best friend had just moved away. I hoped Hector and I would become good friends. He was going to come to my house today for the first time.

Then a fly flew toward me. It was ugly and scary. I think all flies are ugly and scary. In fact, I think all insects are ugly and scary. Even ladybugs. Please don't tell anyone that.

The ugly and scary fly looked like it was headed right to my face, maybe even into one of my eyeballs.

I ran away as fast as I could. I was so scared that I didn't watch where I was going.

I ran right into Graceville. Graceville is
the part of the playground that Grace Chang
named after herself. She reserved it every day for
herself and her friends, Emma G. and Emma J.
She wouldn't let anyone else use Graceville.

The school rules don't allow reserved seating
or standing. But no one wanted to argue with
Grace Chang.

Though Grace Chang is a short, skinny girl, she is evil. Also, she has very long fingernails.

Grace grabbed the back of my jacket. "How dare you set foot in Graceville!" she shouted.

THE EVIL RULERS OF GRACEVILLE

"How dare you," said Emma G., who was standing on one side of Grace.

"How dare you," said Emma J., who was standing on the other side of Grace.

Then Grace pushed me down really hard.

I grabbed onto something to ease my fall.

But the fall did not ease.

I heard a ripping sound.

Then I heard Grace shriek.

Then I fell on my butt really hard.

I realized this day was one of the worst days ever in my entire life.

Then it got worse. Grace yelled, "Zeke 'the Freak' Meeks, you just destroyed my backpack! Emmas, hold him down. I'm going to find our teacher."

Emma G. and Emma J. each put a foot on my chest so I couldn't get up.

By the way, my real name is not Zeke the Freak Meeks. It's Ezekiel Heathcliff Meeks, which is a pretty bad name. But it's not as bad as Zeke the Freak Meeks. Everyone at school besides Grace calls me Zeke, which is a pretty good name.

At the time, I was not thinking about my name. I was thinking that Emma G. and Emma J. needed to clean their shoes.

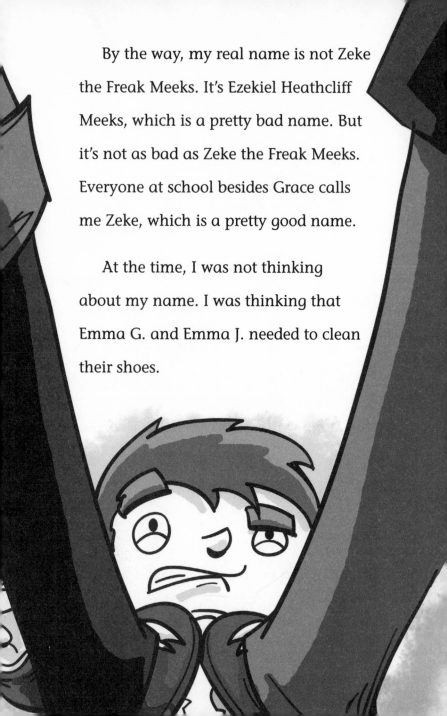

Emma G. had gum on the bottom of her shoe. Emma J. had dog poop on the bottom of her shoe. Since they had their feet on me, I now had gum and dog poop on my shirt.

I was also thinking about the ugly and scary fly that was buzzing over my head.

Hector Cruz came over. He looked down at me and asked, "What happened?"

I didn't want to admit that I was scared of flies. I also didn't want to admit that little Grace Chang had pushed me down. I also didn't want to admit that two other little girls had me pinned to the ground. So I said,

I'M JUST RESTING HERE.

Grace came back with our teacher, Mr. McNutty. Grace was crying. She has an amazing ability to cry whenever she wants to. One day, she may be famous as an actress in sad movies, or for having the world's longest fingernails. But today, she was just an evil third-grade girl who knew how to fake cry and had long nails.

"Zeke Meeks destroyed my backpack," Grace cried to our teacher.

"It's not destroyed," I said.

Grace cried even harder. "The." She sobbed. "Strap." She sobbed again. "Is." She sobbed again. "Broken."

Then she cried and shouted "Oh, oh, oh, oh" a bunch of times. Her fake crying was really impressive.

Emma G. and Emma J. went over to Grace and hugged her.

This allowed me to stand up.

This allowed Grace to blow her nose on my shirt. My shirt now had gum, dog poop, and Grace's snot on it. I told you this was one of the worst days ever in my entire life.

GROSS!

When the teacher wasn't looking, Grace smiled at me.

Hector Cruz told Grace, "If you ever cried for real, no one would believe it. You're just like The Boy Who Cried Wolf. Except you're not a boy. And you don't talk about wolves. Okay, you're just The Girl Who Cried."

"You hurt my feelings!" Grace fake cried. When the teacher wasn't looking, she winked at Hector.

Then she said, "Zeke should pay for a new backpack for me."

"No," I said.

"Yes," Mr. McNutty said.

"That's not fair," Hector said.

"And he probably should sit in the classroom during lunchtime," Grace added.

"No," I said.

"Yes," the teacher said.

"That's not fair," Hector said.

"And he should give me fifty dollars for a new backpack," Grace said.

"No," I said.

"Yes," the teacher said.

"That's not fair," Hector said.

"That's settled," the teacher said.

"But Grace pushed me down. I just grabbed her backpack to ease my fall," I said.

"Sweet little Grace Chang would never push anyone," Mr. McNutty said. Then he walked away.

Grace waved her hand in front of my face. "Do you see these fingernails?" she asked.

"Of course I do," I said. "They're right in front of my face. Plus, they're so long that everyone on the playground can see them."

"People in airplanes and astronauts in space can probably see them, too," Hector said.

WHY IS SHE SO MEAN?!

"Thank you," she said.

"That's not a compliment," Hector said.

"My long fingernails are very useful. If you don't give me fifty dollars for a new backpack, I will use my long nails to scratch your face off," Grace said. "Now get out of Graceville."

Emma G. and Emma J. said, "Now get out of Graceville."

So we did.

The ugly and scary fly followed us.

Still One of the Worst Days Ever in My

NOW YOU
UNDERSTAND WHY!

BUGS IN CLASS

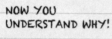

ENTIRE LIFE,
But with Some Hope at the End
of This Chapter

I didn't think one of the worst days ever in my entire life could get any worse. I was wrong. It did. We had a science lesson. I despised science. Science lessons were either hard or boring or both. Usually both. I despised science even more than I despised bedtime.

Today, science was especially despicable. We had to study cockroaches.

Did I tell you the one thing I am extremely afraid of? Oh, yes, I just reread the first chapter. I'll remind you in case you forgot. I'm terrified of insects of all kinds. On my list of scariest things in the universe, insects are the eleventh. The first ten are Grace Chang's long fingernails.

I didn't want anyone to find out I was afraid of insects. They could tease me or put insects in my lunch bag. Or they could tease me *and* put insects in my lunch bag.

So when Mr. McNutty projected a picture of an ugly and scary cockroach on the wall, I didn't scream or run out of the room. But it was very hard not to do both of these things.

Mr. McNutty handed each of us an article about cockroaches.

He said, "Read the article and look at the picture of the cockroach. Then draw a cockroach, label the parts of its body, and list five facts about cockroaches."

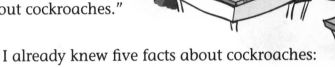

I already knew five facts about cockroaches:

1. They are ugly and scary insects.

2. I have nightmares about them crawling on my face.

3. There should be a law banning all cockroaches and other insects.

4. They terrify me.

5. There is no way I could do a science project about cockroaches.

Then Mr. McNutty told everyone to work with the person next to them.

Victoria Crow sat next to me. She said, "I'm the smartest kid in third grade."

I said, "I know that."

"Everyone knows that," Victoria said. "I'll take charge of this project. Zeke, you draw the cockroach. You don't need to be smart for that. I'll read the article, write down the most important facts about cockroaches, and label the parts of the cockroach's body."

"Okay," I said in a shaky voice.

My hands shook, too.

They shook so much that I couldn't draw a cockroach.

Victoria read the article and circled important cockroach facts.

I was still shaking.

She started writing.

I was still shaking.

She finished writing.

I was still shaking.

She snatched the paper from my desk and said, "You're no use." Then she drew the cockroach herself.

I despised science even more than I despised shopping for underwear.

We were the first ones finished with the project. Actually, Victoria was the first one finished with the project. All I had done was shake.

Mr. McNutty looked it over. "It's perfect," he said.

"Of course it is. I'm the smartest kid in third grade," Victoria said.

"You and Zeke make a good team," Mr. McNutty said.

"No we don't," she said.

"This is good practice for the science fair," he said.

"Science fair?" I asked in a shaky voice.

"Science fair," Mr. McNutty repeated. Then he said loudly, "Class, we are going to have a science fair. Everyone will do a science project."

I raised my hand and asked, "Can I team up with Victoria again?"

"You and Victoria make a good team," our teacher said.

"No we don't," Victoria said.

"But everyone is going to do his or her own project," the teacher said.

Victoria squealed,

I muttered, "I despise science even more than I despise lima beans."

Mr. McNutty said, "Anyone who doesn't do a science fair project will miss recess every day for a week."

I put my head on my desk.

Then Mr. McNutty said, "The person with the best project will get a fifty-dollar prize."

I lifted my head. "I will win the prize," I said.

"No you won't," Victoria said. "I'm the smartest kid in third grade. I won the class speech contest, essay award, and spelling bee. I will win the science fair prize, too."

"No you won't," I said. I wanted to win the contest. It was true that Victoria Crow was the smartest kid in third grade.

It was also true that I despised science even more than I despised being sent to my room. It was also true that the only contest I had ever won was a burping contest. But I would work as hard as I could to do a prize-winning science project.

I had to win. If I didn't get the fifty-dollar prize and give the money to Grace Chang, she would rip my face off.

MY LIFE STINKS LIKE
THIS MOLDY PIECE
OF CHEESE

One of the Worst Days Ever in My Entire Life Gets Even WORSE

After school, my mom said the same three words she always said: "How was school?"

It was horrible, terrible, and awful. As I mentioned, it was one of the worst days ever in my entire life. But I answered my mom's question with the same three words I always said: "School was fine."

Our dog jumped on me. His name is Waggles. Believe me, I did not choose that dumb name for him.

I had wanted to call him Rocko or Brutus or Hulk. But I was outvoted by my sisters and my mom. They thought the name Waggles was cute.

Waggles is a great dog, but he isn't cute. He's a beast with scruffy fur, droopy ears, yellow teeth, and a drooling problem. Today, my little sister, Mia, had put a big pink bow on his head and a pink ballet tutu around his stomach. Even in pink, Waggles wasn't cute.

I petted him. "Your outfit is so wrong," I said.

WHAT IS
WAGGLES
WEARING?!

He slobbered all over me. I think that meant he agreed with me.

Mia was not paying attention to us. She was watching *Princess Sing-Along* on TV. She sang along with the princess on the show. Actually, she screeched along with the princess on the show. They screeched, "Don't stain your nice clothes, la la la. Don't pick your nice nose, la la la. Don't let out a slurp, la la la. Don't let out a burp, la la la."

Mom let me use the computer. Mr. McNutty had given us a list of websites with science projects on them. I scrolled through the projects.

Aha! I found one that looked like a sure science fair winner. I looked up from the computer and said, "Mom, I'm going to make powerful explosive dynamite."

"No, you're not," she said.

"Why not?" I asked.

She said something, but I couldn't hear her. Mia was shrieking along to the TV show. "Wipe your tush after a number two, la la la. Make sure you get off all the poo, la la la."

"What did you say?" I asked Mom.

"Wipe your tush after a number two, la la la. Make sure you get off all the poo, la la la," Mia repeated.

"I wasn't talking to you," I said.

"Oh," Mia said. "Well, Zeke, make sure you wipe your tush after a number two anyway."

"Thanks for the advice," I told Mia. "Now what did you say, Mom?"

"I said you're too young to make dynamite," Mom said.

I sighed. "How old do I have to be?"

"Ninety-six," she said. "Find a safer project."

Finally, I found an experiment that looked good and safe. I could find out which type of cheese grew the most mold. Cheese was popular at my school. So was gross stuff like mold.

So my project probably would be popular, too.

I got slices of American, cheddar, and Swiss cheese from the refrigerator. I put them each on a plate. Then I labeled each slice and predicted which type of cheese would spoil first. I chose American, because I knew some spoiled American kids. I didn't know any Swiss kids or cheddar kids.

My older sister, Alexa, came into the kitchen and asked me something.

"What?" I asked.

Mia and Princess Sing-along were shrieking, "Brush your teeth two times a day, la la la. Or they'll get stinky and gray, la la la."

"I asked you what you were doing," Alexa said.

"It's a science experiment to see what kind of cheese spoils the fastest," I told her.

She wrinkled her nose. "Eww. Gross. I don't want smelly, moldy cheese in my house."

"Zeke has to do this project for school," Mom said.

"Yeah," I said.

Alexa stomped into her bedroom and slammed the door.

"Make sure you leave the cheese in a place that Mia can't reach," Mom said.

"Okay," I said. I put the plates of cheese on a high shelf in the kitchen.

Then Hector came over. He asked, "Can I borrow your jacket. I need it for my science project?"

"Sure," I said. "What science project are you doing?"

"It's a secret," he said.

"Mine isn't a secret. Do you want to see it?" I asked.

"Sure," he said.

I took down the plates of cheese, put them on the kitchen counter, and explained my project.

"It will be so cool once the cheese gets green and brown splotches all over it," Hector said.

"I know. And I can't wait until it starts stinking," I said.

"Eww. Gross," my sister Alexa called out from her room.

My sister Mia sang, "Even in a rush, la la la, don't forget to flush, la la la. Wash your hands to kill the germs, la la la. Otherwise you could get worms, la la la."

"Eww. Gross," Alexa yelled again.

Hector and I went into my room and played with my LEGOS.

We had just finished building a robot-horse when my mom called, "Ezekiel Heathcliff Meeks! Get in the kitchen right now!"

I walked into the kitchen. Hector followed me.

Waggles was lying on the floor. Next to him was a mound of dog barf. The barf was orange and yellow. It had chunks of cheese in it.

My sister Alexa walked by. She plugged her nose and said, "Eww. Gross. Eww. Gross. Eww. Gross."

My sister Mia came into the kitchen. She reached down and said, "I want to play with the goop."

"Get away from that. It's Waggles's vomit," Mom told her.

Mia plugged her nose and said, "Eww. Gross."

"Clean that up right away, Ezekiel," Mom said. "I warned you to be careful with the cheese."

"You warned me to keep it away from Mia. You didn't mention Waggles," I said. Mom glared at me.

Hector said, "I guess I should go home now."

"Sorry, Hector," I said.

"It's okay." He walked away, taking my jacket with him.

But it wasn't okay. Hector wouldn't want to be my friend now. My science project was ruined. Mom was mad at me. And I had to clean up a big pile of dog barf.

On the BRIGHT SIDE,

Waggles Didn't Throw Up Again

The next day, I went on the computer again to look for a new science experiment.

Waggles lay next to me. My sister Mia had clipped purple butterfly barrettes to the fur on his back. "I'm sorry you look so silly," I told him.

Mom said, "Don't do any more projects that could make Waggles throw up."

I spent a long time trying to find another project. I despised science even more than I despised homework. I double despised science homework.

It was hard to concentrate. Princess Sing-Along was on again. Mia and the princess shrieked, "Worms are very cute, la la la. It's nice to meet them, la la la. It's okay to touch them, la la la. But you shouldn't eat them, la la la."

I didn't think worms were cute. I didn't want to meet them. I didn't want to touch them. And I would never, ever, ever eat them.

I clicked on an experiment called "Exploring Quicksand." It came with a recipe to make something like quicksand. It seemed easy. There were only three ingredients: cornstarch, water, and food coloring.

It would be fun to see how fast things sank in quicksand.

And I didn't think Waggles would eat it.

I brought out the little tub Mia used to take baths in. I put it on the kitchen floor and mixed the ingredients in it. The quicksand I made looked really cool.

MASTER AT WORK!

Next, I searched for things to test in the quicksand. I chose three objects for my experiment.

First, a tennis ball that Waggles played with sometimes. It was old and covered with dried dog drool. Second, I chose a plastic block from the back of my closet. I hadn't used it in years. I hadn't cleaned my closet in years. Third, I found a sparkly gold bracelet that had been lying on the bathroom counter. Mia probably used the bracelet for dress-up games.

I took the objects into the kitchen. Then I dropped them, one by one, into the quicksand. I counted how many seconds it took for each object to sink all the way in.

I let out a big yawn. This experiment wasn't cool enough to win the science fair contest. I would have to look for a better project tomorrow.

I took the ball, block, and bracelet out of the quicksand. They were sticky and dirty and smelled weird. I threw them in the kitchen trash can.

It was no big deal. Waggles had other balls to play with. I never used my old blocks. And Mia had other toy bracelets to use for dress-up games.

Next, I put the quicksand down the sink.

Then Mom shouted, "My bracelet is missing!"

Uh-oh.

She ran into the kitchen. She said, "It's my very favorite bracelet."

Uh-oh.

"Where did you see it last?" I asked. I hoped she wouldn't say the bathroom counter.

"The bathroom counter. I left it there when I washed my hands," she said.

Uh-oh.

"What does the bracelet look like?" I asked. I hoped she wouldn't say it was gold and sparkly.

"It's gold and sparkly," she said.

Uh-oh.

I peered into the trash can and said, "I'll look for it."

"Why are you peering into the trash can?" Mom asked.

"No reason," I said.

She walked to the trash can and peered into the trash can.

Uh-oh.

Mom screamed, "Ezekiel Heathcliff Meeks!"

I guessed Mom was angry, based on several clues: She screamed, she called me by my full name, and her face turned bright red.

Then she said, "I'm angry."

"I know," I said. "I'm sorry. I thought the bracelet was one of Mia's toys."

"What is that horrible gunk on it?" she asked.

"Homemade quicksand. And some stuff that was in the trash can. I think some of yesterday's dog barf got on it," I said.

"Take my bracelet out of the trash can and clean it!" Mom screamed so loudly that Waggles whimpered and put his paws over his face.

Mom wasn't just angry. She was furious.

Fortunately, I was able to get all the quicksand and dog barf and other trash off the bracelet. Unfortunately, it took me three hours.

I finished just in time to brush my teeth, change into my pajamas, and go to bed.

Then I lay awake half the night worrying about the science fair and Grace Chang's fingernails.

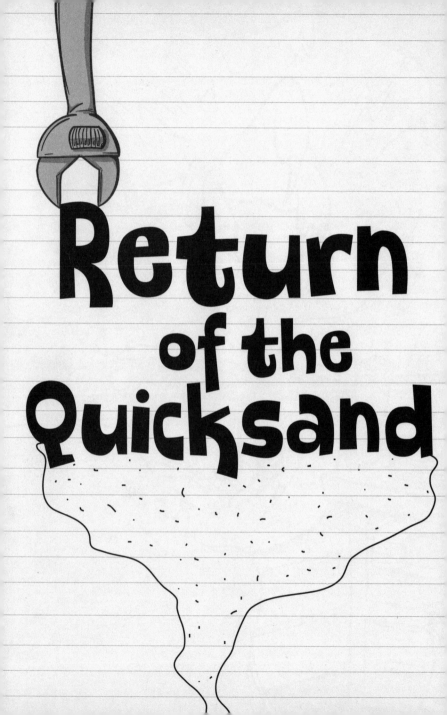

As I was leaving the classroom for recess the next day, I noticed that Victoria Crow was still at her desk. I said, "I can't believe you have to stay inside during recess. How did you get in trouble?"

"I didn't get in trouble," she said. "I want to skip recess so I can work on my science project."

I couldn't believe anyone would choose to miss recess in order to do a science project. I despised science even more than I despised Grace Chang.

"I'm not just the smartest kid in third grade. I work the hardest too," Victoria said. "I'm going to win the prize money."

I could believe Victoria would win the prize money. I probably wouldn't win. I didn't even have a science project yet.

I walked out of the classroom.

As soon as I got outside, someone smacked me in the face with a snowball.

"Gotcha!" Grace Chang said. "Does your face hurt now?"

"Yes," I said. "It's killing me."

She giggled her evil giggle.

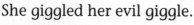

Then she said, "Soon you won't have to worry about snowballs hitting your face. Because you won't have a face. My fingernails will rip it off of you. I sharpened my nails last night just for you."

"Please don't bother," I said.

"It's no bother. I enjoy it," Grace said. Then she skipped off to Graceville.

Hector came up to me. "What are you going to do about Grace Chang?" he asked.

"Sneak into her house when she's sleeping and clip her nails?"

"That's a thought," he said.

"Or I could win the science fair contest and give her the prize money."

"That sounds easier," Hector said.

"What science project are you doing?" I asked.

"It's a secret," Hector said.

I frowned. "My project is such a secret that it's even a secret from me."

"I have an idea," Hector said. "You can show what snow can do."

"Grace already showed me. It can get packed into a ball and thrown at my face."

"That's not the only thing snow is good for. Or bad for," Hector said. "Did you know that salt turns snow even colder than normal?"

"You can combine snow with salt," he added, "and use the freezing cold mixture as an ice cream maker. I can help you try it after school."

"Everyone loves ice cream. That might be a science fair winner. Thanks," I said.

Hector came over after school. We started working on the science fair project right away.

Mom said, "You'd better not make a mess."

"We won't," I said. "And we'll keep Waggles away from the ice cream."

When Waggles heard his name and ice cream in the same sentence, he drooled extra hard. Some of it landed on the flowery shirt that Mia had dressed him in.

Hector and I put vanilla, sugar, and the cream Mom used for her coffee in a plastic bag. Then we shook the bag to blend everything.

But we'd forgotten to seal the bag. Vanilla, sugar, and cream landed all over us and on the floor and on Waggles.

"Don't make a mess!" Mom called out from the bathroom.

Hector and I cleaned up the mess as fast as we could.

We started the experiment all over again. "We used up all the cream for my mom's coffee. We can't make any more mistakes," I told Hector.

We sealed the bag very tight. This time, everything stayed in the bag when we shook it.

Then we put snow and salt in a jar. We covered the jar tightly and took turns shaking it for five minutes. We both had sore arms, but we now had our ice cream maker.

Next, we put the bag in the jar. Then we sealed the jar tightly again.

We were supposed to shake it for another fifteen minutes. We took turns, trading off after every minute.

The jar felt more and more heavy. My arms felt more and more tired. But I didn't complain. I didn't want Hector to think I was weak.

Then I noticed Hector wincing and rubbing his arms. I asked, "Is this hard for you?"

He didn't answer. Instead, he asked, "Is it hard for you?"

"A little," I said. A burning hot streak of pain shot through my arm.

"It's a little hard for me, too," Hector said. At least that's what I thought he said. He was gasping so much I had trouble hearing him.

"Should I try to get help?" I asked.

"Okay," Hector gasped.

I called out, "Help!"

My mom and sisters rushed into the kitchen. Mom was soaking wet, with shampoo bubbles in her hair and a towel wrapped around her. "I just ran out of the shower. What's the urgent emergency?" she asked.

"We need help shaking this jar to make ice cream."

She glared at me.

Alexa said, "I'll help you."

"Thank you," Hector said.

"But you have to let me eat the ice cream," she said.

"Me too," Mia said.

"Me too. But don't make a mess," Mom said again.

"Okay," I said.

My mom and sisters took turns shaking the jar until the ice cream was done.

It looked delicious.

"I get to try it first," Alexa said. She filled a big bowl with ice cream.

Then Mom took some for Mia and her.

Hector and I got what was left: one spoonful of ice cream. We had to share that spoonful. And we could barely move our arms. But the ice cream was delicious.

After we finished eating, Mom said, "That was tiring. I'm going to make myself some coffee. I really need it."

"We used up all your cream for the ice cream," I said.

She glared at me. "Make sure you clean up."

"I will," I said. I brought the ice cream bowls to the kitchen sink and turned on the faucet.

But the water didn't go down the drain Instead, it filled the sink.

NOT ANOT
MESS! UG

"Stop. You're making a big wet mess. Something must have gotten stuck in the sink," Mom said.

She tried to fix the sink with the plunger. It didn't work.

Then she put vinegar, baking soda, and hot water down the drain. The sink was still clogged.

"Trying to fix the sink is like doing a science experiment," I said.

Mom glared at me again. "I despise science experiments," she said.

Finally, Mom crawled under the sink and took apart the pipes. She peered into the bottom one. "I found the problem" she said. "Did you throw the quicksand down the sink yesterday?"

"Yes, but it wasn't thick enough to clog the drain," I said.

"The quicksand dried out. Then it hardened. Then it clogged the drain," she said.

"Oh. Oops."

"I told you not to make a mess!" Mom shouted.

"I need to go home now," Hector said.

Mom was mad at me. Hector would probably never want to come over again. But I had a good project for the science fair.

The EVIL GIGGLER STRIKES AGAIN

The next morning started out great. I had a wonderful dream in which I ate homemade ice cream and watched Grace Chang sink in a large vat of quicksand.

My radio alarm clock woke me. The DJ said today might be the warmest November day ever in Massachusetts. I loved sunny days. And I was glad the snow would be too slushy for Grace to hit me with more snowballs.

I was especially glad that I had found a great project for the science fair tonight. I hummed a happy tune as I got ready for school.

I was humming during breakfast when my sister Mia said, "Hey, that's a Princess Sing-Along song."

I clapped my hand over my mouth.

She said, "You were humming one of my favorite Princess Sing-Along songs. Put on a sweet smile, la la la. It's always in style, la la la."

"I didn't know that," I said. "Oh, well." I kept humming the happy song.

I stopped humming when I saw Grace Chang waiting for me at school. Her two friends, Emma G. and Emma J., stood behind her.

Grace waved her hand in front of my face.
Her monstrous fingernails dangled near my
eyes. She said, "Look. I painted my fingernails
red, the same color as blood. Now people won't
notice when your face blood gets on my nails."
Then she giggled her evil giggle.

Emma G. and Emma J. also giggled. But their
giggles didn't seem as evil as Grace's. Nothing
seemed as evil as Grace Chang's giggle.

Grace grabbed the front of my T-shirt. "Zeke the Freak Meeks, you owe me fifty dollars," she said.

"I'll get it to you tonight, after the science fair," I said.

"If you don't, you'll lose your face," she said. Then she giggled her evil giggle again. She stomped her foot into a big puddle of melted snow, getting me soaking wet. Then she stomped away.

Emma G. and Emma J. giggled their not evil giggles again and stomped their feet into the puddle, too. But they didn't get me wet. They both fell into the puddle.

Hector and I helped them up.

AREN'T WE NICE?

"Your giggles and feet stomping need a lot of work," I advised them.

"You can practice by giggling into a tape recorder and stomping your feet in front of a mirror," Hector advised them.

They ran off toward Graceville.

After they left, Hector asked me, "Are you okay?"

"Yes. But I'll be a lot better once I win the science fair prize tonight and give Grace the fifty-dollar prize," I replied.

"How are you going to make snow ice cream? The snow is almost all melted away," he said.

Yikes! I hadn't even thought of that. I told Hector, "Say goodbye to my face. This is the last day of its life."

My happy mood had vanished.

FEROCIOUS Gas,
a FLYING HAIRPIECE,
and FIGHTING FISH

I went on the computer as soon as I got home from school. I had only a few hours to find a new science project. A wind turbine project looked cool. But it called for a drill bit and needle-nose pliers. An electronic tester project looked cool, too. But that required wire strippers and insulated jumper leads. I didn't even know what those things were.

I put my head on the desk. I despised science even more than I despised spelling tests.

I would never find a project. Mr. McNutty would make me miss a week of recess. Grace Chang would tear off my face. I probably couldn't go to recess anyway if I didn't have a face.

Waggles came over to me. He wore a T-shirt that said "Perfect Angel." He'd gotten drool all over it.

I patted his head and told him, "I forgive you for eating my cheese experiment and barfing it up. I just wish I could find a new project."

Then I returned to my computer search. Most of the projects I saw were much too hard. I didn't have time to experiment with polymerase chain reactions, dinoflagellates, or genomics. I didn't even have time to learn what they were.

Finally, I found a project. It required only a can of soda. I doubted I'd win the science fair with it, but at least it was something.

My whole family went to the science fair. When we got to the school auditorium, I walked over to Hector and his family.

My mom and sisters followed me.

My sister Alexa suddenly smiled. She rushed up to Hector. "Ooh, Hector, I didn't know you had an older brother," she said. Then she turned to Hector's brother. "And what a handsome brother you are. I feel like we were meant to be together."

Hector's brother smiled back at Alexa. He said, "I feel like we were meant to be together, too."

I frowned and said, "I feel like throwing up."

Mom said, "Don't make a mess."

Mia sang a Princess Sing-Along song. "Don't throw up in your nice bed, la la la. Run to the bathroom instead, la la la."

"Did you find a new science project?" Hector asked me.

"Yes," I said. "And now that it's the night of the science fair, you can tell me what project you're doing."

He shook his head. "It's still a secret."

Every person in our class had to go onstage and talk about his or her science project. Rudy Morse went up first. He said, "I need help from the audience for my experiment. Everyone seated in the first three rows, please move back. It's for your own safety."

After they moved, Rudy said, "For my project, I wanted to learn how far the human fart can travel. To help answer this scientific question, I recently ate a half-gallon of kidney beans."

Then he turned his back to the audience, bent over, and let out a giant fart.

He turned toward the audience again. "Can you smell that?" he asked.

"Yes," someone shouted.

STINK BOMB!

"How about the people in the back of the auditorium? Can you smell that fart?" he asked.

"Unfortunately, yes," someone in the back of the room shouted.

"Everyone in Massachusetts can probably smell that," another person said.

"It's disgusting," one of the parents said.

"Repulsive," Mr. McNutty said.

"Gross," a girl said.

People were coughing all around me, so it was hard to hear what else was said.

I thought Rudy's experiment was cool.

Laurie Schneider shared her project next. She had made the wind turbine I saw on the computer. It looked great.

I whispered to Hector, "I bet she'll win the contest."

Laurie turned on the wind turbine. It was really loud. The wind from the turbine spread Rudy Morse's fart stink all over the auditorium.

Mr. McNutty shouted, "Enough of that!"

"What? Did you say 'I love that'?" Laurie shouted back.

"Turn it off!" he shouted.

"Did you say 'Turn it up'?" she shouted back. "Okay, if you say so." Then she flicked a switch. The wind turbine got louder and faster.

Mr. McNutty rushed to the stage. The wind turbine blew his hairpiece off his head.

Mr. McNutty's hairpiece flew off the stage and across the auditorium.

It landed in Chandler Fitzgerald's project, a fish tank containing Siamese fighting fish.

The fish got angry at the hairpiece and attacked it.

Hector whispered to me, "I didn't know Mr. McNutty was completely bald."

I whispered to Hector, "I didn't know that, either. I changed my mind. I don't think Laurie Schneider's wind turbine will win the contest."

Mr. McNutty announced that there would be a short break. Then he opened all the windows to get rid of the fart smell. He borrowed Laurie Schneider's wind turbine to dry off his hairpiece. It had holes in it from the Siamese fighting fish attack. Also, it smelled fishy.

Finally, it was my turn to show off my science project. I went onstage and shook a can of soda as hard as I could. I asked the audience, "What do you think will happen when I open this?"

"It's going to explode all over the place and make a totally awesome mess!" Rudy Morse yelled.

"Please don't make any more messes, Zekey," my mother said.

"Zekey is a babyish name," Victoria said.

"Be quiet, Vickywicky," Hector said.

While everyone was busy talking, I turned the soda can around in a slow circle and tapped my fingers against the sides of it. Then I yelled,

This Project Is a DISASTER

Everyone stared at the soda can in my hand. Everyone, that is, except my older sister and Hector's older brother. They were staring at each other.

I opened the can. There was a tiny, little bitty fizzing noise. But there was no explosion. The soda stayed inside the can.

"Is that it?" Rudy Morse asked.

"That's it," I said.

"Bummer. I wanted to see a gigantic explosion that made an enormous mess all over the place," he said.

"I didn't," Mr. McNutty said.

"Me neither," Mom said. "I've had enough of messes."

"I'll explain the science behind what just happened," I said. "Shaking a can makes the soda inside it form bubbles. These bubbles are actually dissolved carbon dioxide gas. Opening the can makes the bubbles escape, usually in a loud and messy explosion."

"Yeah! Loud, messy explosions!" Rudy Morse yelled.

I held up my hand to quiet him. Then I said, "I tapped the sides of the can before I opened it. This made the bubbles move to the top. Then when I opened the can, there was very little soda to block the bubbles' escape. So the soda didn't explode."

Everyone clapped. Except Rudy Morse, who booed me, and my older sister and Hector's older brother, who were busy staring at each other.

TRUE LOVE?
YUCK.

My project had turned out well.

You may be wondering why this chapter is titled "This Project Is a Disaster." Well, this chapter isn't over yet.

Grace Chang raced onstage with some soda cans. She said, "That project is too easy. Anyone can do it. Watch." She shook one of the cans. Then she tapped it.

Just as she was about to open it, I cried, "Stop!"

"Zeke the Freak Meeks, you're not the boss of me," she said.

I jumped away from her.

She opened the can.

Rudy Morse cheered.

It exploded all over: in her hair, on her nose, down her body, and over her shoes. The soda also landed on the floor all around Grace. Grace screamed.

I told her, "You have to tap the sides of the can. You tapped the top of it."

"I'll try again," she said. She started shaking another can of soda.

"Stop," I said.

She kept shaking the can.

"Stop," Mr. McNutty said. He rushed onstage.

She kept shaking the can.

"I'll do it right this time," she said. Then she tapped the sides of the can.

"Stop," I said again.

Then I jumped away again.

Grace opened the can.

The soda exploded all over the place again.

Rudy Morse cheered again.

This time, only a little soda got on Grace.

Most of the soda landed on Mr. McNutty. He cried, "Grace Chang! You have ruined my brand new cashmere sweater!"

"But I did the experiment just like Zeke did it," she said.

"You used a can of diet soda. Tapping doesn't work on diet soda," I said. "Scientists aren't sure why. It might be because diet soda has artificial sweetener in it, or because it has more carbon dioxide gas in it."

"Your soda stained my brand new cashmere sweater!" Mr. McNutty screamed at Grace. "You now owe me one hundred dollars for a new sweater."

I covered my mouth, but I couldn't hide my laughter.

I looked over at Hector. He was covering his mouth and laughing, too.

Now do you see why this chapter is called "This Project Is a Disaster"? My science project was a disaster for Mr. McNutty and Grace Chang.

But it was a lot of fun for me.

MY Teacher's FAKE HAIR and Other SCARY GROSS Stuff

SCARY GROSS,
Like this nasty-
looking spider.

9

After Grace Chang mopped up all the soda from the stage, Chandler Fitzgerald showed off his science fair project. He walked onstage with his fish tank. It was full of Siamese fighting fish. It was also full of Mr. McNutty's false hair.

Chandler said, "My project was ruined by Mr. McNutty's flying hairpiece." Then he left the stage and returned to his seat.

Next, Grace Chang brought up large poster boards filled with charts and graphs. She pointed to one of the posters. "This is . . . um . . . um . . ." She looked at her parents.

Her mom mouthed something.

"What?" Grace asked.

Her dad mouthed something.

"I can't hear you," Grace told her parents. "What is my project about?"

Her parents went onstage and explained Grace's project to the audience and to Grace.

"It's obvious that Grace's parents did all the work," my mom told me. She looked straight at me and said,

Then the parents of Emma G. and Emma J.
went onstage. They talked about their daughters'
projects, just like Grace's parents had.

Mom told me again that she was proud of
me.

Owen Leach showed off his experiment next. He said, "For my project, I studied how a spider builds its web." Then he held up a gigantic picture of a spider in a web. It was terrifying.

I fled to the bathroom. I didn't return until Owen and his terrifying picture had left the stage.

Victoria Crow explained her science project by using a PowerPoint presentation she had made and a book she had written. "I will describe my experiment in simple terms," she said. "I analyzed the optimal method to control bacteria, utilizing various disinfectants."

Then she talked for a long time about lab cultures, petri dishes, agar, and other things I didn't understand. If those were the simple terms, I sure wouldn't understand the hard terms.

Smartest kid in 3rd grade

After Victoria finished, Mr. McNutty came onstage and shook her hand. He said, "Excellent work. Your project is more like a college student's. You may have found cures for major diseases."

Victoria smiled and said, "Being the smartest kid in third grade comes in handy. Keep me in mind for the fifty-dollar prize tonight."

I just rolled my eyes and said,

Guess Who Won

the Science Fair Prize

Hector was the last person to go onstage. Finally, his secret science fair project was no longer secret. He said, "I collected fingerprints just like real detectives do. I took a set of fingerprints from Zeke Meeks' jacket."

So that was what he needed my jacket for.

"I sprinkled talcum powder on the back of the jacket," Hector continued. "Then I wiped off the excess powder with a small paintbrush."

"Next, I put tape over the area and lifted off the fingerprints. Then I stuck the tape over a sheet of dark paper."

Hector held up a piece of paper with fingerprints on it. It looked really cool.

Then Hector said, "I used the same process to lift fingerprints from Grace Chang's desk. These are her fingerprints."

He held up another piece of paper with fingerprints on it. That looked really cool too. The fingerprints seemed exactly like the prints he'd taken from my jacket.

Hector said, "I studied both sets of fingerprints. It is obvious they both came from Grace Chang. She denied pushing Zeke Meeks. But her fingerprints are on Zeke's jacket."

Grace ran onstage. She said, "Hector is a big fat liar. I would never push anyone."

Hector said, "You are the one who's lying. I am neither big nor fat. And I'm not a liar. The fingerprints are scientific evidence that you pushed Zeke Meeks. After you pushed him, he grabbed the strap of your backpack to ease his fall."

"I'm not a liar, and I never push people. I'm so mad at you!" Grace screamed.

Then she pushed Hector.

Everyone in the audience gasped, except for my older sister and Hector's older brother. They were too busy staring at each other.

Mr. McNutty ran onstage. He said, "Grace, you owe Zeke an apology. And you owe me one hundred dollars for a new cashmere sweater. Zeke doesn't owe you anything."

"Not fifty dollars for a new backpack?" I asked, just to be sure.

"Absolutely not," Mr. McNutty said. Then he turned to Hector and said, "That was a terrific presentation. One of the best."

"Do I win the contest?" Hector asked.

"The winner of the science fair prize is Victoria Crow," the teacher said.

Everyone clapped, except for my older sister and Hector's older brother, who were busy staring at each other.

Victoria walked onstage. She said, "I knew I'd win. I'm the smartest kid in third grade."

"And the most annoying kid in third grade," I whispered to Hector.

Mr. McNutty gave Victoria a plaque and a gift certificate.

"I thought the winner got fifty dollars," I said.

"Yes. A fifty-dollar gift certificate to spend at Science Products R Us, the science equipment store," Mr. McNutty said.

"Hooray!" Victoria shouted. "That's my very favorite store. There's nothing more fun than shopping for test tubes and chemical compounds."

I could think of some things more fun than that: Playing handball, watching TV, and eating candy. Even brushing my teeth would be more fun than shopping for test tubes and chemical compounds.

Victoria said, "I know just what I'll buy at the science equipment store: an insect farm."

I gulped. "Did you say insect farm?" I asked Victoria.

She nodded.

"Yes. It's a big clear box full of insects. But don't worry. I'll bring it to school to share with the class."

"Did you say 'share with the class'?" I asked.

Victoria nodded. "Everyone will get to touch the creepy crawlers."

"Did you say 'creepy crawlers'?" I asked.

Victoria nodded. "You can let them creep and crawl all over your body. Except for the poisonous insects."

"Did you say 'poisonous insects'?" I asked.

Victoria nodded. "Don't worry. Only one of the insects will kill you. The others will just give you purple rashes, giant sores, and brain clots."

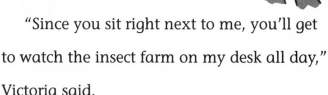

I opened my mouth to ask her something else, but I was too scared to speak.

"Since you sit right next to me, you'll get to watch the insect farm on my desk all day," Victoria said.

I wondered if I could move to a new seat.

Or move to a new classroom. Or move to a new school. Or move to a new city. I wondered if I could move to a new planet that had no insects on it.

Mr. McNutty said, "There's a second-place prize, too. The winner of a ten-dollar gift certificate to the Candy Palace store is Hector Cruz."

I cheered loudly.

"There's also a third-place prize," Mr. McNutty said. "The winner of a five-dollar gift certificate to Candy Palace is Zeke Meeks."

I cheered even more loudly.

When the science fair ended, my mom hugged me. She said, "I'm so proud of you, Zeke. You worked hard and found a great project. You did very well tonight."

"I'm proud of you, too," my little sister said. "I will celebrate your win by putting my prettiest bows and barrettes on Waggles."

"Are you proud of me, too?" I asked my older sister.

She didn't answer. She was too busy staring at Hector's older brother.

I turned to Hector. "Thank you for using your science project to prove that Grace pushed me down."

"You're welcome," he said. "And thank you for letting me come to your house and do projects with you. It was fun."

"But most of my experiments failed. And my mom yelled at me," I said.

Hector shrugged. "We have exciting adventures at your house. And you always try your hardest. I'm glad you're my friend."

"I'm glad you're my friend, too," I said.

"Let's go to the candy store," Hector said.

I smiled. "Cool."

Hector smiled. "Cool."

Then I said, "Maybe we can do more experiments together, too. Some of those science projects tonight looked really fun. I used to think I despised science, but now I like it."

"Do you like science even more than you like candy?" Hector asked.

DO YOU DESPISE SCIENCE?
(And other really important questions)

Write answers to these questions, or discuss them with your friends and classmates.

1. Do you despise science? Why or why not?

2. Me and my classmates did tons of different science fair projects. Which one was your favorite? (It better not be Grace Chang's!)

3. Describe the coolest science project you can imagine. Could you actually do it?

4. How do you feel about bugs? (Obviously, the correct answer is, "I hate bugs!" But be honest.)

5. How can I keep my mom from getting annoyed with me? Do you have any advice?

BIG WORDS
according to Zeke

ARTIFICIAL SWEETENER: Sort of like fake sugar. It tastes sweet, but it doesn't rot your teeth.

AUDITORIUM: The huge room in our school where shows, concerts, and other things parents care about are held. Also, the huge room that Rudy Morse stunk up with his fart science project.

CASHMERE: The super-soft wool fabric that Mr. McNutty's precious sweater was made out of. I guess it must be pretty dainty.

COMPLIMENT: Something nice you say about someone or something. It makes you feel really good.

CONCENTRATE: Think really hard so you can get something done or understand something better. It is impossible to concentrate when Princess Sing-Along is making your ears bleed.

DESPICABLE: Terrible, horrible, awful things that you should never have to deal with are despicable. For example, bugs and science fair projects.

DESPISED: If you hated something more than anything you have ever, ever, ever hated before, then you actually despised it.

DISASTER: A big, huge accident or mistake that usually leads to other big accidents and mistakes. Think of my quicksand science project, Laurie Schneider's wind turbine, and Grace Chang's shook-up soda can.

DISGUSTING: Things that make you go, "EW!" like Princess Sing-Along, most girls, and, according to my mom, Rudy Morse's science project. (See auditorium.)

ELECTRONIC: Things that are powered by electricity are electronic, and, obviously, awesome.

MONSTROUS: When things (Grace Chang's fingernails) are completely awful, huge, and evil, they are monstrous!

REPULSIVE: Very gross, yucky, pukey, sickening . . . well, you get the idea. (See disgusting.)

Make Your Own Quicksand

My quicksand experiment was awesome . . . until I ruined my mom's bracelet and clogged up the sink with it. Here are directions to make your own quicksand. (Just ask your mom first, keep her stuff away from it, and DO NOT pour it down the sink!)

What you need:

- box of cornstarch

- 1-2 cups of water

- your choice of food coloring (optional)

- large mixing bowl

- mixing spoon

What you do:

1. Pour one-quarter of the cornstarch into the bowl. Add 1/2 cup of water. Stir.

2. Continue to add cornstarch and water a little at a time. You want the cornstarch to be about as thick as honey. Use the whole box of cornstarch and 1-2 cups of water in all.

3. Now check out how the cornstarch feels. Move your hands through it. Move them slowly. Then move them quickly. Is there a difference in how it feels?

4. Push your whole hand into the quicksand, and try to pull it out. What happens?

5. Now drop a small plastic toy into the quicksand, then try to pull it out. What happens?

If you want to make your own ice cream, like Hector and I did, download directions in my activity kit at

capstonekids.com/characters/Zeke-Meeks

AWESOME HAI[R]

CHARMING SMILE

COOLEST TH[IRD]
GRADER YOU['LL]
EVER MEET!

WWW.CAPSTONEKIDS.COM